THIS ONE 'N THAT ONE

in

Splat!

The Tale of a Colorful Cat

JANE SEYMOUR and **JAMES KEACH**

illustrated by
GEOFFREY PLANER

G. P. Putnam's Sons   New York

Text copyright © 1998 by Jane Seymour and James Keach
Illustrations copyright © 1998 by Geoffrey Planer
All rights reserved. This book, or parts thereof, may not be reproduced
in any form without permission in writing from the publisher,
G. P. Putnam's Sons, a division of Penguin Putnam Books for Young Readers,
345 Hudson Street, New York, NY 10014.
G. P. Putnam's Sons, Reg. U.S. Pat. & Tm. Off.
Published simultaneously in Canada.
Printed in the United States of America.
Designed by Marikka Tamura. Text set in Gill Sans.
Studio: Mike Goddard and David Trotman.
Library of Congress Cataloging-in-publication Data
Seymour, Jane. Splat! the tale of a colorful cat /
Jane Seymour and James Keach; illustrated by Geoffrey Planer.   p.   cm.
Summary: When Big Jim Cat is left in charge of his kittens, the results of
the painting project he suggests are not quite what he expected.
[1. Cats—Fiction. 2. Father and child—Fiction. 3. Painting—Fiction.]
I. Keach, James. II. Planer, Geoffrey, ill. III. Title IV. Series PZ7.S5235Tj   1998
[E]—dc21   98-4788   CIP   AC   ISBN 0-399-23309-1
1 3 5 7 9 10 8 6 4 2
First Impression

To
Kris and John,
Kalen, Katie, Jenni, Sean, Thea, Erica,
Nina, Tom and Fizzy,
our inspirational friend Christopher Reeve,
and Jan of course!

And all the kids and all the kits around the world!

It was a different sort of Sunday morning.
The Malibu cats had to get up extra early.
Lady Jane had to go shopping.
Jenni Clevercat had to buy a book.
Katie Tomboycat had to play a game.
Sean the Surfercat had to hit the waves.
KK Coolcat had to meet his band.

THIS ONE and **THAT ONE** did not have to go out extra early. But they did get up extra early, and that meant so did their sleepy old dad, Big Jim cat.

The night before, Big Jim had been quite
certain that he could look after the kittens
without Mom; but on Sunday morning
he wasn't so sure anymore.
First he put **THIS ONE**'s pants
on **THAT ONE**.
Then he put **THAT ONE**'s pants
on **THIS ONE**.
Then he put **THIS ONE**'s pants
on **THAT ONE**'s head.

Big Jim tried to make breakfast. He managed to get some corn flakes into the bowls.
He managed to get some of the corn flakes into **THIS ONE** and **THAT ONE**, and they managed to get the rest of the corn flakes all over the kitchen.
Big Jim managed to clear up the mess; well, some of the mess.
"Oh, boy!" said Big Jim. "You kits are a real pawful."

"Dad, Dad, what can we do?" said **THIS ONE**.
"Dad, Dad, we're bored," said **THAT ONE**.

Then Big Jim looked up at the clock.
Oh, no! It was still only half past nine!
No one would be back till lunchtime!

Big Jim scratched his head with his paw.
Then he scratched his paw with his head.
"Let's think of something fun to do.
What would Mommy do?"

"Mommy does painting!" shouted the kittens.
"LET'S PAINT!" shouted **THIS ONE**.
"LET'S PAINT!" shouted **THAT ONE**.
"But...we don't have any paints," said Big Jim.
"We can use Mommy's paints!" yelled the kittens.

Big Jim thought it was a bad idea;
he even *knew* it was a bad idea.
But somehow he found himself standing on a chair
getting Mom's paints out of the closet.

Big Jim got out the aprons and spread out
some old newspapers.

"Now, kits—no mess at all; comprendes?
No paint on YOU, and no paint on YOU, and no
paint on the FLOOR. Promise?" said Big Jim.
"We promise," said **THIS ONE** and **THAT ONE**.

"What can we paint, Dad?" asked **THIS ONE**. "Don't be furbrained—use your imagination. Pablo Picatso and Henri Catisse didn't ask their dads for ideas." Big Jim yawned.

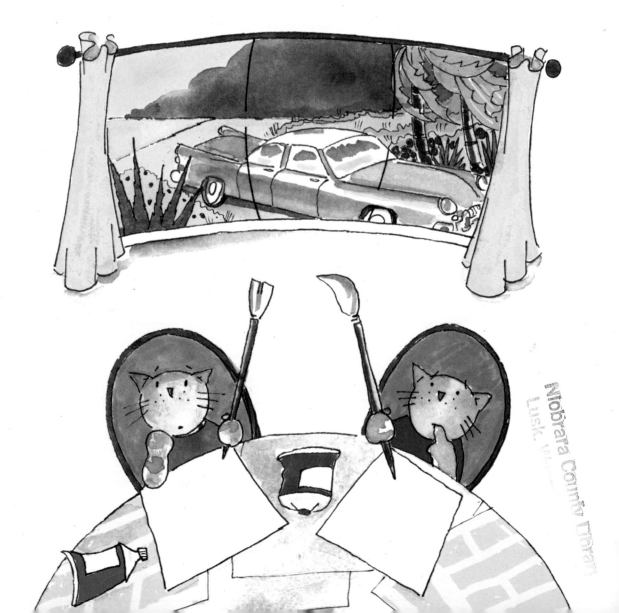

"We can't think of anything to paint, Dad,"
said **THAT ONE**.
"Why not paint a car?" said Big Jim.
"Paint a car?" said **THAT ONE**, amazed.

"OK then, why not paint the garden?"
"Paint the garden?" said **THIS ONE**, astonished.
"You guys are hard to please,"
said Big Jim sleepily.

"Why not paint me?" Dad sighed.
"Yes, paint me, and then you can show
Mom when she gets back.
And make it colorful.
But no paint on YOU, and no paint on YOU,
and no paint on the FLOOR," said Big Jim,
and he closed his eyes.

THIS ONE looked at **THAT ONE**.
THAT ONE looked at **THIS ONE**.

THIS ONE mixed some yellow and green paint.
THAT ONE mixed some purple and pink paint.

"OK, Dad—we're ready
to paint you," they said.
But Big Jim did
not answer.
"I think Dad's keeping
still so we can paint him
easily," said **THIS ONE**.

So, very quietly, **THIS ONE**
painted Dad's face red and
his whiskers orange
and his nose blue.

Then **THAT ONE** painted
his paws white and
his tummy with brown stripes
and his legs with little red spots.

"Mom's going to be really
happy when she sees how
well we painted Dad,"
whispered **THAT ONE**.
"Zzzzz," snored Dad.

The kittens heard Lady Jane's car pull up
and ran outside to meet her.
"Mom, Sean, KK, Jenni, Katie, come
see our painting!"shouted
THIS ONE and **THAT ONE**.

Lady Jane opened the door and dropped
the shopping in surprise.

There on the chair slept a very
well painted Dad!
"And we didn't get any paint
on US!" said **THIS ONE**.
"And we didn't get any paint on
the FLOOR!" said **THAT ONE**.

"Oh dear!" said Lady Jane,
looking white.
"Zzzzzz," snored Dad,
looking colorful.

Some blue for his nose,
And spots of red;
Some green for the hair
On a furry head
Some white for his paws,
And pink on his heart.
Old Big Jim
Is a work of art!